For Gloria Molinaroli, her cat Homer,
and the St. Johnsbury Athenaeum
R. L.

For Polydor
A. W.

First edition 2011

Library of Congress Cataloging-in-Publication Data

Lindbergh, Reeve.
Homer the library cat / Reeve Lindbergh ; illustrated by Anne Wilsdorf. —1st ed.
p. cm.
Summary: A cat's quiet life is disrupted one day when a window is broken,
and after several frustrating attempts to find a suitable place,
he winds up in the perfect spot.
ISBN 978-0-7636-3448-3
[1. Stories in rhyme. 2. Cats—Fiction.] I. Wilsdorf, Anne, ill. II. Title.
PZ8.3.L6148Ho 2011
[E]—dc22 2010048130

11 12 13 14 15 16 SCP 10 9 8 7 6 5 4 3 2 1

Printed in Humen, Dongguan, China

This book was typeset in Mrs. Eaves.
The illustrations were done in watercolor and collage.

Candlewick Press
99 Dover Street
Somerville, Massachusetts 02144

visit us at www.candlewick.com

HOMER
THE LIBRARY CAT

REEVE LINDBERGH

ILLUSTRATED BY ANNE WILSDORF

CANDLEWICK PRESS

Homer was a quiet cat,
quiet as a mouse.
A quiet lady lived with him
in a quiet house.

The lady went away each day.
Homer stayed at home.
He sat beside the window,
peaceful, all alone.

He played with yarn and feathers.
They made no noise at all.
When he heard a bird, he purred.
Mice played with his ball.

Homer was at home alone
the day he heard a CRASH!
He jumped right out the window
and landed in the trash.

The trash cans fell and BANGED and rolled,

and Homer ran away.

Where was the quiet lady?

What a noisy day!

The post office was right next door;
Homer went inside.
But Hope and Noah had to sneeze,
and Homer had to hide.

Inside the fire station,
he found a quiet place
right beneath the ladder,
a cozy, cat-size space.

CLANG! CLANG! The fire bell rang.

A fire! A fire in town!

Five fit firemen jumped right up.

One quick cat jumped down.

Homer ran and ran and ran
down to the railroad track.
He found an empty boxcar
and jumped up in the back.

A locomotive came along
with engineer and crew.
Just as Homer fell asleep,
the whistle blew, CHOO! CHOO!

Homer ran back into town
and through an open door,
into a quiet building,
across a quiet floor.

He heard a quiet voice he knew.

He saw a rocking chair.

There was the quiet lady!

And children everywhere.

"Homer!" said the lady.
"What are you doing here?"
Homer jumped into her arms
and purred into her ear.

The boys and girls loved Homer.
Homer loved them back.
He slept right through the stories
but woke up for the snack.

Now Homer is a Library Cat—
he goes there every day.
What do the children think of that?
"It's purr-fect!" they all say.